HAMSTER PRINCESS

Of MICE and MAGIC

Dial Books for Young Readers

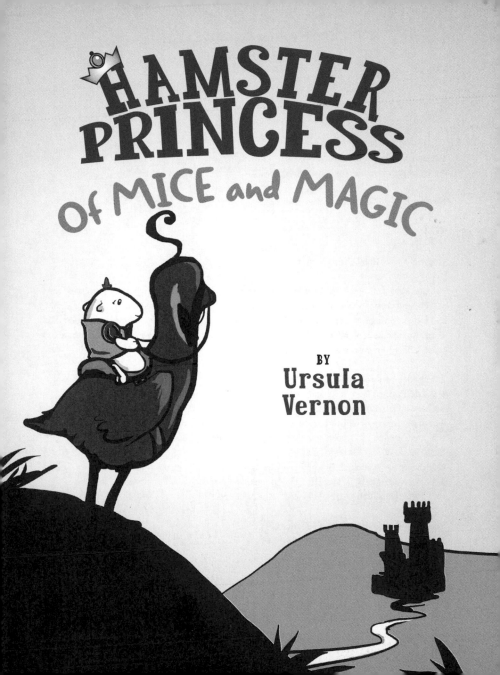

HAMSTER PRINCESS
OF MICE and MAGIC

BY
Ursula Vernon

Dial Books for Young Readers
Penguin Young Readers Group
An imprint of Penguin Random House, LLC
375 Hudson Street
New York, New York 10014

Library of Congress Cataloging-in-Publication Data   Vernon, Ursula.
Hamster Princess 2 : of mice and magic / by Ursula Vernon.   pages cm.
Sequel to: Harriet the invincible.
Summary: "Harriet Hamsterbone sets out to reverse the curse on twelve mice princesses who are forced to dance all night, every night"— Provided by publisher.
ISBN 978-0-8037-3984-0 (hardcover)
[1. Princesses—Fiction. 2. Blessing and cursing—Fiction. 3. Hamsters—Fiction.
4. Humorous stories.] I. Title. II. Title: Of mice and magic.
PZ7.V5985Han 2016   [Fic]—dc23   2015006966

Printed in the United States of America
10   9   8   7   6   5   4   3   2   1

Design by Jennifer Kelly
Text set in Minister Std Light

To the many
friends of Rooster
the Paladin.
Weasel Invicti!

HAMSTER PRINCESS

Of MICE and MAGIC

HARRIET

HER FAITHFUL BATTLE QUAIL, MUMFREY

CHAPTER 1

Once upon a time, in a kingdom just over the next hill, there lived a fierce warrior hamster named Harriet Hamsterbone.

Harriet's parents were a king and queen, which meant that she was a princess by definition, but Harriet herself was more interested in slaying monsters than in most of the traditional occupations of princesses.

Up until a few months ago, she had been invincible, owing to a fairy curse gone awry, but now she was merely very, very stubborn.

She was also a bit cross because she had to give up cliff-diving. Cliff-diving is a marvelous sport if you are invincible, but not so marvelous if you can actually break every bone in your body doing it.

"I don't know, Mumfrey," she said. "If I go back home, Mom is going to try to get me to take deportment lessons. I don't think I can stand to balance a book on my head again."

"Qwerk . . . ?" said Mumfrey, which is Quail for "Yeah, but what are you gonna do?"

"I need an adventure," said Harriet. "I need to do something! I'm nearly twelve and a half! Do you know how long it's been since I fought an ogre?"

"Qwerk," said Mumfrey, which is Quail for "Seven and a half weeks."

THAT ONE DIDN'T COUNT. IT WAS BARELY EIGHT FEET TALL.

The problem, Harriet decided, was that she was bored. The monsters had all heard about her.

Many of the ogres had given up eating people and taken to vegetarianism in a big way so that she wouldn't show up and start whacking them with her sword. Jousting contests now had rules stating that if you'd won in the last three years and you were a hamster whose name started with *H*, you had to sit out and let somebody else try. She'd been away from home for three weeks, just trying to find something to do, and there was *nothing*.

IT'S LIKE THE WHOLE WORLD IS CONSPIRING TO KEEP ME BORED.

"Qwerrk," said Mumfrey, but he said it under his breath. Mumfrey knew that in a land containing dragons, ogres, dark knights, and fearsome curses, there was nothing half as dangerous as Harriet when she was bored.

Harriet was trotting along on Mumfrey's back when she heard a voice from the side of the road.

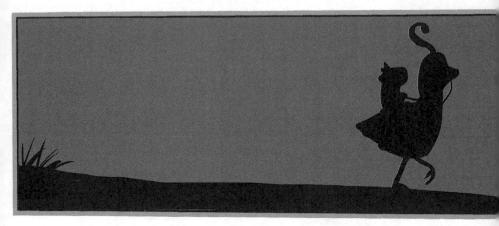

"Good warrior, will you not stop and help a wretched old soul?"

The hamster reined in her quail and eyed the speaker suspiciously.

There was a little old lady sitting on a rock by the side of the road. She was a shrew, but the smallest, oldest, most bent-over shrew that Harriet had ever seen.

"Please, mighty warrior, won't you spare a crust of bread for a starving old woman?" asked the shrew. Her voice was weak and creaky and sounded like an old door hinge in the rain.

Now, Harriet had had more than her fair share of experience with fairy god-mice and wicked rat-fairies and witches and curses.

She was also nobody's fool.

Nobody talks like that in real life, she thought to herself. *And I'm about a six-hour ride from the next village, which means that this old woman has been doing some hiking to get here.*

You should be polite to people on general principle, of course. But if you happen to be wandering through a magical land, and a little old lady asks you for help, you should be *extremely* polite to her, just in case. Otherwise you may well wake up with earthworms falling out of your mouth whenever you talk, or various other suitably awful fairy punishments.

"Sure," said Harriet, sliding off Mumfrey and rummaging in her saddlebags. "I'd be happy to.

"Let's eat our lunch together."

She had two cheese sandwiches and some carrot sticks set aside for lunch. Just to be on the safe side, she gave the old shrew the lion's share of the carrot sticks, along with a sandwich.

She also made sure that her sword was within easy reach. You never could tell with fairies.

YOU'RE SO KIND TO A HELPLESS OLD LADY, DEARIE.

UH-HUH.

The shrew ate her sandwich and most of the carrot sticks and also the cupcake that Harriet had been planning on eating for dessert. Then she belched. Loudly.

"Thank you, dearie," she said, patting Harriet on the knee. "That was very gracious of you."

"I'm glad that I could help," said Harriet.

The shrew tapped her nose with a long claw.

KINDNESS DOES NOT GO UNREWARDED. DO YOU KNOW WHAT I AM, LITTLE HAMSTER?

A FAIRY.

ACTUALLY, I'M A FAI—

There was a brief, awkward pause.

"I *see*," said the shrew, in a much less feeble voice. "Figured that out, did you?"

"Sorry," said Harriet. "You're a bit far out of town for a real little old lady. And you rather overdid the helpless-old-lady thing. Plus . . ." She cleared her throat. "It's your shadow. You haven't got one."

"Bless it!" growled the old woman, and whistled sharply.

Her shadow, which had been cavorting with the flickering shadows of some willow leaves, jumped up and came sliding hurriedly across the grass.

It fastened itself to her heels and hunched down, looking sheepish.

"Silly old thing! You cut it loose once, and it gets in the habit of wandering off." The shrew scowled.

WELL, I *WAS* GOING TO SEND YOU ON A QUEST . . .

I FIGURED.

"You keep being so sharp, you're liable to cut yourself," said the shrew, looking cross. "Fine. Off with you, then. I'll wait for the next hero."

Harriet sighed. That was the problem with fairies. Some of them were extremely touchy.

"Well . . ."

"It's possible that I might have another cupcake in here somewhere," said Harriet. "I was going to save it for Mumfrey, but if you're going to send us both on the quest . . ."

"Qwerk!" said Mumfrey, annoyed. That was *his* cupcake!

"It's a *good* quest," said the shrew. "I wouldn't want to waste it on just anybody."

IT'S BIRDSEED AND CHOCOLATE FLAVORED . . .

QWERRRRK!?

"Fine!" said the shrew fairy, snatching the cupcake and devouring it in three bites. (Shrews are almost always hungry.)

She licked frosting off her whiskers and patted the rock beside her.

"Now, sit down, dearie, and I'll tell you the story of the Twelve Dancing Mouse Princesses . . ."

CHAPTER 2

Far away from here (said the shrew fairy), in a great kingdom to the west, lived a royal family of mice. The mouse king had twelve daughters.

Their names were January, February, March, April, May, June, July, August, September, October, November, and December, because the king

had that sort of relentlessly logical mind. (He also had two sons named Solstice and Equinox, but they'd fled the kingdom as soon as they were old enough. People like the mouse king are difficult to live with.)

More than anything in the world, it was said, the princesses loved to dance.

They danced fox-trots and tangos and square dances and reels. They danced waltzes and quadrilles and jigs and cotillions. They could dance any dance ever invented. A constant stream of dancing instructors went up to the palace and taught the twelve mouse princesses everything they knew, and then went home again, exhausted.

What the dancing instructors had noticed was the state of the shoes worn by the twelve mouse princesses.

The shoes were made of silk, of course, in pink and ice white and sky blue, and they were carefully fitted to the feet of every princess like a glove is fitted to a hand.

("Yuck," said Harriet, who thought silk shoes were ridiculously impractical.)

And every morning, the silk shoes were worn completely through. There were holes in the heel and holes in the toe, as if the princesses had been dancing all night.

Eventually the king noticed as well. First he was very confused, and then he started to get angry. The oldest princess was thirteen years old and the youngest was eight, and they were going through an immense amount of shoes.

The royal shoemakers were summoned and threatened with terrible punishments for making substandard footwear, but the shoemakers had sterling reputations and produced several dozen professional ballerinas who testified at their trial that these were very fine shoes indeed. The fault did not lie in the shoes.

And if the shoes were not at fault, that meant the princesses were dancing their shoes off every night.

This is considered very strange behavior for princesses, and the mouse king did not approve of strange behavior.

DO YOU DANCE ALL NIGHT? WHERE DO YOU GO? *TELL ME!*

The mouse king threatened his daughters with terrible punishments. He had them all grounded and doubled their homework and sent them to bed without supper and took away all their toys.

. . . but still none of them said a word.

The mouse king raged and yelled and stomped about the castle, and would have come up with even worse punishments, but the court wizard stopped him. He had been conducting his own experiments and had a few suspicions.

YOUR MAJESTY, THE PRINCESSES ARE CLEARLY UNDER A SPELL. DO NOT PUNISH THEM, BUT RATHER, SEEK HOW TO BREAK IT.
. . . RIGHT. YOU, WIZARD! BREAK THAT SPELL!

I'M REALLY MORE OF A RESEARCH WIZARD. ALSO, I'M RETIRING NEXT WEDNESDAY.

The mouse king sent for other wizards, for knights and heroes and princes, for anyone who could find out where the princesses went at night and how they danced through their slippers.

He offered half the kingdom and the hand of his oldest daughter in marriage if anyone succeeded, so there were quite a number of people eager to try. Stable boys and dishwashers turned up at the palace, hoping to be princes.

But none of them ever succeeded. Most went

away embarrassed. One slept so late that he had to be dumped into the moat to wake him up, and he fell asleep again while talking to the king. He was escorted to the edge of the kingdom and dropped there. On his head.

One or two of the people who tried were never seen again.

The mouse king became extremely grumpy.

THIS IS *NOT* WORKING.

As for what the twelve mouse princesses thought of the matter, nobody was sure. Every night, all twelve were locked into a room of the palace, and none of them would ever say where they went, or how.

And every morning, their shoes were worn away to nothing.

In this very unsatisfactory state of affairs, six and a half years passed.

CHAPTER 3

Harriet listened to the whole story from first to last. Her big pink ears stayed trained on the old shrew, not flicking from side to side to catch the sounds of the forest.

> AND
> THAT IS THE
> STORY . . .

When the fairy was finished talking, Harriet sat in silence.

"Oh, very well," said the shrew. She watched Harriet with bright black eyes.

What Harriet was thinking was, *There's more going on here than she's saying.*

After a few minutes, the hamster princess said, "Did they ever try tying the princesses up?"

"What kind of question is *that?*" asked the shrew, a bit shocked.

"A logical one?" said Harriet. "I mean, if they've tied the princesses up and they got loose anyway, then there has to be someone helping them, right? Why not send them to another castle while they're at it? And they should have tried taking away the shoes and giving them very big stompy boots to see what happened."

(Harriet herself did not usually wear shoes—hamsters don't, unless they're planning on walking through something disgusting—but when she did wear shoes, she preferred very large boots with steel toes and, if possible, spikes.)

NOW WE'RE TALKIN'!

"I was expecting you to be a bit more concerned for the plight of the princesses," said the shrew sourly. "As a fellow princess and all. I don't mind telling you that I'm having second thoughts here."

Harriet shrugged. She had not met very many princesses, and the ones she had met were all rather useless and tended to spend a lot of time brushing their hair and singing duets with little forest animals. It was all very soppy.

"As a fellow *girl,* then," said the shrew. "Since they're under a curse. I'd think you'd remember what that's like."

"Look," said Harriet, "if they're unhappy, they have all my sympathy, okay? But the mouse king doesn't sound like a very nice man. Maybe the princesses *like* dancing. Maybe it's nobody's business where they go."

BEING A HERO
DOESN'T APPEAL TO YOU?
HALF THE KINGDOM
DOESN'T *INTEREST* YOU,
I SUPPOSE?

"I've got my own kingdom in a few years," said Harriet. "And I'm already a hero. Ask any of the ogres. *If* you can find one."

"Fine," said the shrew, sighing. "If you're going to be like *that,* I suppose I'll have to tell you the rest of it."

Harriet examined her fingernails and tried not to look smug.

"It *is* a curse," said the shrew. "All the fairies know about it. There was a write-up in *Fairy God-mouse Today,* but of course no one will tell the mouse king the details."

EVERY NIGHT, NO MATTER WHERE THE PRINCESSES ARE, A DOOR OPENS IN THE FLOOR OF THEIR ROOM.

"Whether they want to or not," the shrew said, "the mice must climb down, down, into the underworld beneath the castle."

AND THERE, EVERY NIGHT, FOR ALMOST SEVEN YEARS, THEY HAVE DANCED.

"And if you tie them up?" asked Harriet again.

"Fine!" said the shrew. "The ropes come untied, if you must know!"

"And if you move them to another castle—"

"Earthquakes. They can't go beyond the wall around the castle grounds, or the whole thing starts shaking and the turrets start falling into the moat. The king keeps guards to make sure they stay on the property, for fear that the castle will fall down."

"Hmmm," said Harriet. She had to admit, that did sound like a pretty powerful curse. "If somebody sleeps in their room—"

"Aha!" said the shrew. She tapped Harriet's knee with one long claw. "Now you've got it. All those knights and heroes and princes and stable boys hoping to be princes—they get three nights. Most of them fall asleep and don't remember what happened, and a few of them have disappeared completely."

TIME IS RUNNING OUT. IF THEY DANCE FOR SEVEN YEARS, THEN THE SPELL WILL FINALLY BE COMPLETED AND THE PRINCESSES WILL BE TRAPPED UNDERGROUND FOREVER. THEY CANNOT WAIT ANY LONGER. THEY NEED A DIFFERENT KIND OF HERO.

Harriet rubbed the back of her neck. It did sound interesting, and she was awfully bored . . .

Still, you didn't just go breaking other people's curses because you were bored. The princesses might love to dance, and they might not thank her for getting involved.

"I don't know . . ."

The shrew scowled.

"I didn't want to say this," she said. "But if you do not help the princesses, Harriet Hamsterbone, then your own kingdom will be in peril. I have seen the future, and if the princesses are not freed, then the name of Harriet Hamsterbone shall be written in dust and in a handful of generations, the line of hamster kings shall end!"

She sat down with a thump.

"Written in dust?" said Harriet. "Like . . . somebody swept up some dust and wrote my name in

it? That's just weird. Why would
I be scared of that?"

The shrew groaned. "It's a *metaphor.* Like your
name won't matter, because people won't remember it."

Harriet looked unconvinced.

"Maybe you should focus on the bit with the
hamster kings coming to an end," said the shrew.

"Right . . ." said Harriet. "How many generations are in a handful, exactly?"

"What?"

"It's not a very *scientific* measurement, is it?"

The shrew put her long snout in her hands.

"Like, my parents are one generation, right? And I'm two, and if I have kids—which I suppose could happen, in theory, someday—that's three. If a handful is three generations, then we're already there and that's bad! But if a handful is like forty-five generations, then we're only a fifteenth of the generations involved, and I sort of feel like the other fourteen-fifteenths need to take care of themselves. I can't be responsible for *everybody*."

"I'm just saying," said Harriet. "So how many generations are we talking about?"

"Not that many," said the shrew.

"And how does this work exactly?"

The shrew rubbed her forehead. "Look, the future isn't a straight line or anything. Probably one of the princesses will marry somebody who was planning on invading the hamster kingdom and she'll talk him out of it. Or maybe she'll invent a better quail saddle and one of your descendants who was going to fall off his quail and break his neck won't. Futures are

squishy. All I know is that if you don't do this, your kingdom will suffer.

"I'm doing you a favor here," said the fairy.

"Right," said Harriet, climbing to her feet. If the future of the hamster kingdom was at stake, she knew what she had to do. She held out her hand to the shrew. "You've convinced me. One hamster hero, at your service."

CHAPTER 4

Harriet was in an excellent mood.

The sun was shining, the birds were singing, and she had a quest to follow and some fellow princesses to save. The notion that failure would mean the eventual end of her own kingdom did not bother her. Failure, in Harriet's world, happened to other people.

"This is just what we need, Mumfrey," she said. "I get to save the future kingdom *and* it gets me out of the castle again!"

"Qwerk," said Mumfrey bitterly. He was still sulking about his cupcake.

They made good time down the road. In fact, they made entirely *too* good a time down the road.

"I'm pretty sure we should be about a week away from the palace," said Harriet. "But that sure looks like it down there."

"Qwerk," said Mumfrey, which was Quail for "Fairy work. I don't trust it."

"Me neither," said Harriet, "but here we are anyway."

She rummaged around in Mumfrey's saddle-bags, and found two packages that she was pretty sure hadn't been there before.

FAIRIES JUST CAN'T LEAVE WELL ENOUGH ALONE, CAN THEY?

Mumfrey was thrilled. His box contained not one but *two* chocolate-and-birdseed cupcakes.

QWER-*RK!*

Harriet opened her package.

Instead of cupcakes, Harriet's box contained a strange, slippery gray fabric.

She shook it out. It looked like a cloak, but there were no clasps. It was a circle of fabric with a hole in the middle for her head and a large hood.

Harriet could tell, just by holding it, that it was magical. It made her whiskers tingle. She pulled it on.

A Poncho of Invisibility is not quite as good as a Cloak of Invisibility, but they're cheaper and easier to sew. Harriet had to readjust the folds several times to make sure that her feet didn't become visible.

Mumfrey scowled. He didn't like invisibility. There was a nasty bit when the poncho was partway on and partway off where he could see Harriet's innards. The princess was his best friend and he loved her very much, but he still didn't want a view of her giblets.

"Right," said Harriet, stashing the poncho back in her saddlebags. "I get it. I'm supposed to go invisible and follow the princesses. No need to draw me a map or anything." (It was, frankly, a better plan than she had been working on, which had involved disguising herself as a mouse princess. Hamsters do not look very much like mice, and Harriet was a terrible dancer.)

"C'mon, Mumfrey," she said. "Let's get curse-breaking."

CHAPTER 5

Princess Harriet arrived at the castle and went immediately to the stables with Mumfrey. Stables tell you a great deal about how a kingdom is run. If they're warm and dry and cleaned out regularly, that's one thing.

If they're filthy and badly lit and the grain is full of mold and weevils, the odds are good you don't want to spend very long in that particular kingdom. It remained to be seen how the mouse kingdom would measure up.

A hamster came around the corner, wiping his hands. "My apologies, traveler, I was seeing to a—"

He stopped.

He stared at Harriet.

Harriet stared at him.

"Wilbur?!"

"*Harriet?!*"

"A fairy sent me," said Harriet. "Curse on the princesses, needs breaking—well, you know." She waved a hand in the direction of the castle. "Why are you here?"

"They needed a stable boy," said Wilbur. "All the other stable boys went off to try and fix the curse."

"You're a prince," said Harriet.

YEAH, WELL . . .
ALL THE STABLE BOYS WANT
TO BE PRINCES. MAYBE A
PRINCE SHOULD BE A STABLE
BOY FOR A CHANGE.

"Besides," he added, "Heady the hydra's laid an egg and she's gonna have a baby hydra soon, and you know how much they eat. And the basement flooded again."

"You didn't want to try breaking the curse yourself? You'd get half the kingdom . . ."

Wilbur shuddered. "I can't even pay for the kingdom I've *got*. And I'd have to marry a princess," he said. "I am not getting married. I barely escaped marrying *you*."

This might have been insulting, but Harriet felt quite the same way about it. Wilbur was a good friend, but not a *boyfriend*.

She'd first met Wilbur while breaking her own curse, and she knew that his mother's kingdom was very poor. Wilbur had been able to fix the roof with the reward from breaking Harriet's curse, but money was still tight.

He'd had a paper route, but being a stable boy probably paid better. She knew from listening to her father complain that basements were expensive to fix.

"It's wonderful you're here," said Harriet warmly. "You're just the person I need. Tell me everything about the kingdom. Is the mouse king a good man? Are the princesses unhappy? Can I leave Mumfrey here? How good is the birdseed?"

Wilbur held up his hands to forestall the questions. "The stables are fine. The birdseed is excellent. I don't know that much about the king, but I'll tell you everything I know."

THE KING IS *WEIRD*. HE GETS REALLY STRANGE IDEAS.

"He was determined to have twelve daughters named after months. He had a list and he'd cross a name off every time he had another daughter."

"Yikes!" said Harriet. Being a princess was hard enough without being a name on somebody's list.

EVERYTHING IN THE KINGDOM IS THE VERY BEST QUALITY, BUT IT'S TERRIFYINGLY WELL-ORGANIZED.

HOW SO?

WE HAVE TO ALPHABETIZE *EVERYTHING*. YOU PUT BIRDSEED IN FRONT OF ALFALFA AND YOU GET YELLED AT.

"The king will only travel in carriages pulled by quail that match *exactly*. The footmen have to all be the same height and wear uniforms that match the curtains. I've heard the royal bodyguards are actually identical twins. And you'll see about the décor when you go inside." Wilbur shook his head. "It's . . . well, it's something."

Harriet was extremely curious now, but she had one last question. "What about the princesses?"

Wilbur shrugged. "They're okay. Most of them never come down here. I see August sometimes. She has a quail."

Mumfrey looked up, interested.

"A riding quail, not a battle quail," said Wilbur.

"That's okay. Mumfrey started out as a riding quail. He's learned to be a fearsome battle quail now, though!"

"Qwerk!" said Mumfrey, which was Quail for "I am very fierce."

"Does she seem like she's under a curse?" asked Harriet. "The princess, not the quail. Does she act normal?"

Wilbur thought about it. Unfortunately, he didn't know many princesses. August didn't act like Harriet, but then again, who did?

"She seems angry," he said finally. "And sad. Talk to her. You'll see."

CHAPTER 6

Harriet went into the castle by the side door. She was barely through the second set of rooms before she realized what Wilbur had meant about the décor.

Everything matched.

The first room was purple. The walls were painted purple, the drapes were purple, the door frames and tapestries and throw pillows were purple.

The second room was green. The walls were green, the carpets were green, the end tables were inlaid with green marble, and the lamps had green blown glass shades. You got the impression that if there had been a way to make the sunlight coming through the window green, the decorator would have done so.

The third room was blue. The ceiling was blue, the walls were blue, and the decorator had solved the sunlight problem by installing a blue stained-glass window that streamed blue light over the blue carpet on the blue floor.

There was a guard. Harriet thought he was wearing blue, but even if he weren't, his clothes would have *looked* blue. His fur had a bit of a bluish cast, but that was probably the light.

HALT!
WHO GOES
THERE?

PRINCESS HARRIET.
I'M HERE ABOUT THE CURSE.

To his credit, the guard did not say "But you're a girl" or "But you're awfully young" or any of the other regrettable things that people often said to Harriet.

"You'll have to go to the Gray Room," said the guard. "It's down the hall to the left, third door, down the stairs, turn right, up the spiral staircase—"

"Can't you show me?" asked Harriet.

"No," said the guard. "I'm in Blues."

He said this as if it were an obvious statement. Harriet waited politely for a moment and then said, "Yes? And?"

YOU CAN'T GO INTO ANOTHER COLOR ROOM. IF SOMEONE IN BLUES GOES INTO THE PINK ROOM, THEY'D *CLASH.*
THE KING WOULD BE VERY UPSET.

It occurred to Harriet that she was dealing with a very peculiar sort of mind.

"I *see*," she said. "What do you do when you need to go to the bathroom?"

The guard stared at his feet. "We make sure the rooms are cleared, then make a run for it," he mumbled. "But don't tell the king!"

"Wouldn't dream of it," said Harriet, patting him on the arm.

She was wearing blue herself, but no one tried to stop her. Apparently the rule only applied to employees.

After wandering over what felt like half the castle, Harriet found a pale pink room. It was just as overwhelming as all the other rooms, but there was a small mouse in a white dress in it, arranging flowers.

The mouse squeaked and whirled around. A second mouse, who had been staring out the window, turned toward the door.

"Sorry," said Harriet. "I'm looking for the Gray Room. I've been through two Blue Rooms, one Green Room, what I think was two separate Orange Hallways—although I might have wandered into the same one twice—and something that I think was the Magenta Room, except that it was so blinding that I had to close my eyes and feel my way to the door. Can you help me?"

"You're supposed to curtsey," said the mouse by the window. She sounded snotty but also tired, as if being snotty was just a habit by now and she didn't really care one way or the other. "We're princesses."

"Well, that makes three of us," said Harriet, who was not above being a princess when it suited her. "Princess Harriet, at your service."

The mouse at the window looked Harriet over and then turned back to the window. "Our dad's kingdom is bigger." She leaned her head back on the windowsill and appeared to doze off suddenly.

GIVE IT A REST, SEPTEMBER— OH, NEVER MIND . . .

To Harriet, she said, "I'm sorry about my sister. I'm August. It's nice to meet you."

"August!" said Harriet. "You're the one with the riding quail, then?"

"Oh, yes!" August put her hands together. "My dear little Hyacinth! I don't get to ride her as much as I want to. We can't leave the castle grounds . . ."

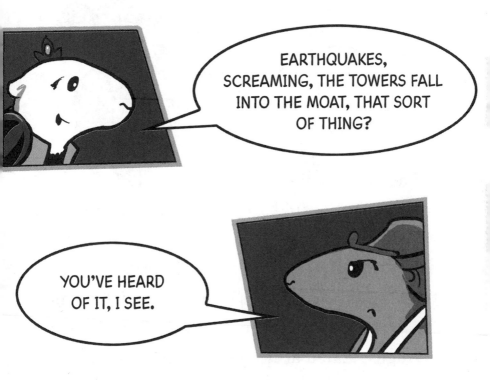

IT'S WHY I'M HERE.

...OH.

This was not the reaction
that Harriet would expect from someone who
wanted their curse broken.

She considered various subtle methods of ex-
tracting information, and then rejected them all in
favor of asking: "Do you *want* your curse broken?"

August stared at her feet. After a moment, she

picked up the flowers and began sliding the stems, one by one, into the vase. The flowers were pink, of course, but their green stems made a welcome break from the pink covering the room.

"Nobody can break the curse," said September, waking up. She blinked a few times and stifled a yawn.

LOTS OF PEOPLE HAVE TRIED. SOME OF THEM DIED.

"I don't want anybody else to get hurt," said August angrily, cramming the rest of the flowers into the vase. "I wish I *wasn't* a princess!"

"Boy, have I been there," said Harriet. She patted August on the shoulder.

The mouse princess looked surprised at the sympathy.

"Come on," she said finally. "I'll take you to my father, the king."

The mouse king sat in the Throne Room, which was several hallways away from the Gray Room.

You could not simply go to the Throne Room. Harriet discovered this when August went to the Gray Room to summon a butler (who wore black) and the butler went through the hallway opening doors.

"If you wear black, you can go to any of the

rooms," August explained. "Black goes with everything and doesn't clash."

"Your father certainly has some *interesting* ideas," said Harriet. She made a mental note to acquire a rainbow-colored hat at the earliest opportunity, and wear it in every possible room to annoy him.

The Throne Room was black and silver. It was twice as large as the one in Harriet's parents' castle, but it seemed nearly empty by comparison.

"Your Majesty," said the butler, bowing, "may I present the Princess Harriet, Slayer of the Wicked Fairy Ratshade, Bane of Ogres, and Champion of the Joust."

"Did you *really* slay a wicked fairy?" whispered August.

"Nah," whispered Harriet. "I just de-magicked her. Last I heard, she had moved to another country and was selling condemned real estate."

The mouse king did not look impressed by any of these titles. He straightened up in his chair, but not by much.

"What brings you here, Princess Harriet?" he asked.

Harriet bowed. She wasn't going to curtsey, even for a king.

"I'm here about the curse, Your Majesty," she said.

There was a lengthy pause.

A rat standing beside the throne leaned forward and whispered something to the mouse king. The king whispered something back. The rat whispered something rather urgently. They both looked at Harriet, then back to each other.

PSST PSSSST PSST

Harriet wondered if she should be offended. Finally the mouse king said, "You're a girl."

"Oh, you're quick, Your Majesty," said Harriet.

The rat cleared his throat, took a step forward, and said, "I believe what His Majesty *intends* to say is that the call for curse-breaking was to *heroes*."

UH-HUH.

...NOT *HEROINES*? ER? YOU SEE?

LOOK, YOU WANT THE CURSE BROKEN OR NOT?

"You really think you can break the curse?" asked the king. "Many men have tried already."

"Had they ever been cursed?" asked Harriet. "And were they slayers of wicked fairies, *and* jousting champions? Because if not, I'm better."

More whispering.

"Very well," said the king. "I suppose we do not need to worry about the details unless you manage to succeed." From his tone, Harriet could tell that he didn't think this was likely. "The rules are simple. You may spend three nights in the hall where the princesses sleep. At the end of three days, you will either tell me how the princesses wear their shoes through, or you will leave the palace—and my kingdom—at once. Is that clear?"

"Yep," said Harriet.

"If you succeed, the reward is half the kingdom and the hand of one of the princesses in marr . . ."

He stopped. He looked at Harriet, who was undeniably a twelve-year-old girl. He opened his mouth and closed it again.

"Half the kingdom and a princess," said Harriet cheerfully. "Got it."

"Do you have any questions?" asked the king.

"Just one," said Harriet. "What would you have done if December had been twins?"

The king didn't so much as blink. "I would have disowned the younger twin. It is a set of twelve, *not* thirteen."

Definitely a peculiar sort of mind. Harriet wasn't sure if she should break the curse or lead a revolution and put one of the princesses on the throne instead.

"Report to the Gray Room tonight," said the mouse king. "You will be taken to the princesses."

"Righto," said Harriet, and left the room without bothering to bow.

CHAPTER 7

Harriet spent the rest of the afternoon making a map of the castle. This was very boring work and required several different colors of crayon, but she was able to find her way to the Gray Room without any trouble.

From the Gray Room, the butler led Harriet up a long spiral staircase and into the princesses' bedroom. They slept in a tower, very high above the ground, to make it extra-hard to break in.

The bedroom was very long, lined with a dozen

beds with iron frames. There were bars on all the windows.

The door was made of iron and had seven locks and seven bars and four combination locks and three chains and a complicated thing made out of spikes. Someone wanted to make *very* sure that door stayed closed.

"This is like prison," said Harriet.

The butler grunted. He shut the door behind her, and she heard the bar grind heavily into place and then the clunks and bangs and clatters of the other locks closing.

She turned and faced the princesses. They were wearing nightgowns and holding each other's hands.

All of them looked sad. Some of them looked angry and sad or bored and sad or tired and sad. Harriet thought that she had never seen so many shades of sorrow in one place.

One or two appeared to be dozing off where they stood. Dancing all night apparently left you very tired in the morning.

"Right!" said Harriet, clapping her hands. "Listen up!"

All twelve of the mice stared at her.

"You all look like you're at a funeral," said Harriet. "I don't blame you. Your father's *very* weird. Also there's this whole curse thing going on. My name's Princess Harriet, and I'm here to break the curse."

(Privately she thought that something would have to be done about the mouse king as well, but that was technically treason, so she kept it to herself.)

"Now then," said Harriet. She decided to find out what kind of princesses these were, and whether they were going to be any help in breaking the curse. "If you could be anything—anything at all, not a princess—what would you be?"

The mouse princesses looked at her as if she'd lost her mind.

"C'mon, don't be shy. I fight ogres. I really want my own pirate ship. What would *you* do?"

It was August who had spoken. Harriet wasn't surprised at all. "Good choice! What else?"

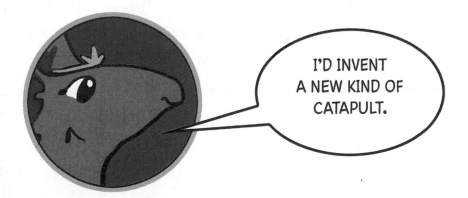

I'D WRITE NOVELS.

I'D GET MARRIED AND HAVE TEN KIDS AND I WOULDN'T NAME THEM AFTER MONTHS OR DAYS OR ANYTHING. THEY'D HAVE REAL NAMES. LIKE SAMANTHA. OR BOB.

"Great!" said Harriet. "Nobody wants to brush their hair and sing duets with forest animals? Good. I can work with that. Except maybe the ten kids thing." She cracked her knuckles. "Now, I gather that you can't tell me anything about the curse."

Twelve mice shook their heads.

"The spell stops you from talking about it, the usual magic stuff?"

Twelve mice nodded glumly.

"But you'd like it broken if possible."

Twelve mice nodded vigorously.

"Does anybody here actually *like* dancing?"

There was a long, long silence.

I USED TO.
NOW I HATE IT.

"December, was it?" asked Harriet. She patted the youngest mouse on the shoulder. "Well, we'll see what we can do."

A small room had been separated from the rest of the bedroom with paper screens. Harriet set her packs down inside it and looked at the bed. Dozens of unsuccessful heroes had slept there.

Probably none of them had a Poncho of Invisibility, though.

She sat down on the bed. In the other room, she could hear the princesses getting ready for bed.

January, the oldest mouse, tapped on the screen. "I brought you some hot chocolate," she said.

"Thanks!" said Harriet. "That's very kind of you."

There was an odd moment as January tried to hand her the mug, and at the same time tried to *not* hand her the mug. Her fingers flexed helplessly on the handle.

Harriet could recognize a spell when she saw it. She took the mug away from the mouse and lifted it to her lips. January watched her closely.

It was the best-smelling hot chocolate that Harriet had ever sniffed. It had nutmeg and cinnamon and spices.

And if it doesn't also have something in it to make me sleep, I will personally eat my sword. Without salt.

August peeped anxiously around the screen frame.

If I don't drink it, January will know that something is up, though. I wonder if she'd be forced to give me another drink.

Harriet drank the whole cup of hot chocolate in one draft and smiled brightly at the mouse princess.

January nodded, took the mug, and left. "Good night," she said from the doorway.

Harriet waited until the princess had left, pulled the chamber pot out from under the bed, and spat the entire cup of chocolate into it.

Everybody forgets that we hamsters have cheek pouches . . .

HAMSTER WITH FULL CHEEK POUCHES

↓

HAMSTER

↓

"Blech," she said under her breath, wiping her whiskers with a handkerchief.

She looked up. August was still watching her.

Harriet winked.

CHAPTER 8

When the door opened in the floor, Harriet was ready.

She had been lying in bed with the blanket pulled up over her shoulders. She was already wearing the Poncho of Invisibility under the blanket. She kept her eyes nearly closed and watched the doorway under her eyelashes.

January came to the door and glanced in.

She was no longer wearing a nightgown. She wore a ball gown with frothy skirts and silken dancing slippers.

"Come on," said a voice. Harriet was nearly sure it was August. "She drank the whole thing. She's out cold."

"Hurry up," said someone else. "My feet are starting to itch!"

"Very well," said January, and turned away.

Harriet could hear the sounds of mice getting changed, and the tapping of their feet. It sounded like some of them were starting to dance already.

She threw the hood over her head and crept to the edge of the screened room.

The door in the floor was just as the old shrew had described it. It yawned open like a mouth, and the mouse princesses walked through it, one by one. All of them were dressed in gowns and wore silken slippers on their feet.

They were beginning to dance as they walked, tapping their toes, bouncing up and down. February and March did a tango the length of the bedroom, without looking as if they were enjoying it much.

August was last. She paused in the doorway and glanced over her shoulder.

"Close the door!" hissed one of the other mice.

Harriet flicked the poncho so that it covered her feet and scurried through the doorway.

There was a long flight of steps down, down, into the dark.

August pulled the door shut. Harriet flattened herself against the wall so that the mouse wouldn't run into her.

As it was, the mouse princess brushed against the poncho anyway. Harriet held her breath.

"What's wrong, August?" one of the other mice called.

NOTHING. CAUGHT MY DRESS ON THE DOOR.

"Hurry!" called January. "We'll be late."

"Heaven forbid we keep them waiting," muttered August. She gathered up her dress and hurried down the stairs.

Harriet went down the stairs behind her, setting her feet down at the same instant that the princess did, just in case anyone was listening and wondering why there was an extra set of footsteps.

The stairs went down and down and down. Harriet's whiskers tingled.

Magic, she thought grimly. Even if the castle had walls thick enough to conceal a staircase in, they were now a long way underground.

Climbing back up is not going to be fun. Poncho of Invisibility or not, if I'm clinging to the walls and wheezing, they'll probably hear me.

The stairs opened suddenly into an enormous cavern. A path made of white stone wound between swaying silver trees, leading across the cavern to a distant river.

Harriet did not know a great deal about trees. There were only so many hours in the day, and she preferred to spend her time studying things that might attack you.

She was pretty sure that normal trees didn't grow underground, though.

The other princesses were hurrying down the path. August trailed after them.

Harriet reached up to a passing tree. The bark was cold under her fingers—cold like metal, not like wood. The leaves appeared to be made of silver foil.

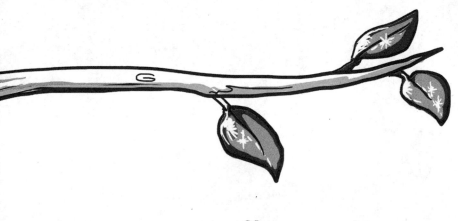

A whole forest made out of metal. This is getting very odd. Somebody spent a long time and a lot of magic building all this down here.

Harriet's whiskers twitched. *Gotta be a witch. Nobody loves forests like witches. If you can't have a forest underground, a witch would build one.*

Harriet had nothing against witches—one of her dear friends was a witch, in fact—but they did have their little quirks.

Still, if I wanted proof that I'd actually followed the princesses, and wasn't just making up a story . . .

She snapped off a twig.

CRACK!

Harriet jumped. The sound of the twig breaking was like a bowling ball being dropped on a tin roof.

All the mouse princesses froze.

Harriet stuffed the twig into her pocket and ran after the mice.

The silver trees became gold trees, the gold trees became diamond, and the black river drew closer and closer.

And if I were not very sensible, I would start breaking off gold and diamond twigs too, and make more noise than an elephant coming through. No way. Either the king believes me when I show him a silver twig or he doesn't.

They reached the river.

The water was as black as ink, and it didn't move like water was supposed to move. Harriet scowled. The last time she'd seen water like this—stuff that was only *pretending* to be water—there had been a squidweight* at the bottom of the lake.

There were twelve boats drawn up on the shore. Standing in each boat was a hooded figure with a pole.

---

*Squidweights are more or less like squid, but they crawl around on land and make puddles out of ink. When things fall in and drown, the squidweight eats them. Harriet's squidweight had been the size of a cow, and defeating it had taken three hours and a snorkel.

"Nothing creepy about *that* . . ." muttered Harriet under her breath.

Each mouse princess stepped up into a boat. The hooded person pushed off from shore with the pole and into the river.

Uh-oh.

Twelve boats, and there's not a lot of room in each one—

January and February were halfway across the river. The rest were pushing off. The only boat left was August's, and only because she had stopped to tie her shoe.

Harriet jumped into the boat just as August stepped in. It nearly overbalanced.

"Whoa!" said the hooded boatman.

"Sorry, my foot slipped," said August.

The prow of the boat was carved into a figurehead, in the shape of a giant earthworm. There was a little bench in the middle of the boat. The mouse princess sat down. Harriet crouched behind her.

An earthworm? That's . . . peculiar. I've seen dragons and swans carved on figureheads, but never earthworms.

The boatman dipped his pole into the water and pushed away from the shore.

The other boats quickly outdistanced them.

"Have you gained weight?" asked the boatman.

"Oh, aren't we tactful?" asked August.

"I didn't mean—"

IF YOU MUST KNOW, I'M WEARING LEAD UNDERWEAR.

Harriet bit her lower lip to keep from laughing.

"You . . . wait . . . *lead underwear?!*" said the boatman.

"It's prescription," said August. "For my back. You know, like copper bracelets when you've got arthritis? Well, if your back hurts because, oh, let's say *you spend every night dancing underground because of a fairy curse,* you wear lead underwear."

". . . I see," said the boatman. "Well, it's not much longer, you know. Another two months and the curse will be finished."

THEN I'M NEVER DANCING AGAIN.

"Only a matter of time," said the boatman.

Harriet wondered whether she'd be able to knock him into the river and grab the pole before he went under.

Funny thing, though . . . the boatman didn't sound any happier about it than August did.

Another two months. Hmm.

The princesses may have two months, but I've only got three days to sort this out.

August put a hand out behind her back.

Harriet slipped one hand from under the Poncho of Invisibility and squeezed the mouse princess's fingers tightly.

Three days should be plenty. I hope.

CHAPTER 9

It took only a few minutes before the boat reached the far side of the river. A dock stretched out, lit with twinkling lights, and the boatman poled the boat up to it and tied it off.

He offered August a hand out of the boat, but the mouse princess ignored it. She climbed out with the maximum amount of kicking and flailing, which covered the motion of the boat as Harriet slipped past her onto the dock, careful to avoid the boatman.

The boatman pulled off his cloak.

Underneath, wearing a tuxedo, was a mole. He had velvety fur and a twitchy pink nose, and he didn't look particularly evil.

Harriet scowled inside the poncho. A mole? Really? That did explain the giant underground caverns and the earthworm boat, but she'd never met a bad mole in her life. Or one interested in dancing.

Come to think of it, she'd never met a mole interested in anything but digging. They liked farming and mining as long as they involved digging, games as long as they involved digging, and singing songs as long as the songs were also about digging.

Moles have a rather one-track mind.

PROBABLY
NOT A HAPPY
MOLE.

HAPPY
MOLE

Harriet followed the mouse and the mole along a pathway lined with more silver trees. Through the tree trunks, she caught glimpses of a lighted pavilion, where the other mouse princesses danced with the moles.

There was an enormous symbol laid in tile on the dance floor. Whenever one of the couples danced over it, the tiles lit with an eerie blue light.

And that's how they're powering the spell, thought Harriet. *Oh, there is* definitely *a witch at the bottom of this.*

Fairies are born magical, and when they do a spell, they draw on their own powers. But witches learn magic, and have to get it where they can. The good ones ask politely.

The bad ones . . .

"The princesses are compelled to dance," muttered Harriet under her breath. "They have to dance, and when they dance over the symbol, it generates magic. Like water running through a waterwheel. So they dance and it powers the spell that *keeps* them dancing . . . and I bet there's some left over for the witch. Right."

She straightened her shoulders. "I've had about enough of this."

She hurried to catch up with the mole and August. She had to wait until they went around a bend in the path and the pavilion was briefly out of sight. Then she took two steps forward, drew her sword, and put the mole in a headlock.

WE'RE GOING TO HAVE A CONVERSATION NOW, BUDDY, AND IF I'M NOT HAPPY WITH THE ANSWERS, I SHALL BE FORCED TO DO SOMETHING UNFORTUNATE.

EEEP!

August, not looking at all surprised, said, "I'll go up to the pavilion and get a drink so that my sisters don't wonder where I am. Then I'll come right back."

She hurried off, dancing as she went.

"See that?" said Harriet. "She's got a good head on her shoulders. Do you?"

The mole said, "Is there an answer that doesn't involve you stabbing me? Because I'd like to pick that one."

"Right," said Harriet. "Sit down here. I'm going to let go of you, but I want you to remember that I've got a sword and I'm standing right here, just in case you have any ideas about calling for help."

...I HAVE NO IDEAS WHATSOEVER.

"Good," said Harriet. "I'm Princess Harriet. I'm here to fix the curse. Now, what's with the curse and the princesses?"

The mole heaved a sigh. "Oh. *That.* That's all my mother's doing."

"I'm listening," said Harriet.

"My mother's a mole witch," said the mole.

"Didn't know moles went in for witchcraft," said Harriet.

"We usually don't. Unless it's dirt related. Mom's . . . special." The mole grimaced. "We think she maybe ate a little too much dirt with lead in it, if you know what I mean."

ANYWAY, SHE HAD TWELVE SONS AND SHE DIDN'T KNOW WHAT TO DO . . .

x 12 = ?

THEN SHE HEARD ABOUT THE TWELVE MOUSE PRINCESSES AND SHE GOT THE BRIGHT IDEA THAT ALL TWELVE OF US SHOULD MARRY ALL TWELVE OF THEM.

Harriet tapped a nail on the hilt of her sword. "And you don't mind that when you dance, you're powering her magic?"

The mole shrugged. "She's not a super-powerful witch or anything. If we dance, she'll use her magic to do the dishes. If we don't dance, we have to do them."

Harriet stared at him.

"Do you know *how many dishes* twelve moles can generate in a day?" asked the mole. "It's apocalyptic. A little magical dancing is way better."

Harriet grunted. A minor witch who had figured

out how to power her magic through other people's dancing.

It didn't surprise her. She knew a number of witches. Most of them were very nice. A few of them, however, were not so nice, and when witches went bad . . .

"What are your names?" she asked. "You and your brothers?"

"Aries, Capricorn, Pisces, Sagittarius—"

"All twelve signs of the zodiac," said Harriet, cutting him off.

"Yep," said the mole. "I'm Gemini."

BOY, DO I KNOW A KING YOUR MOTHER NEEDS TO MEET . . .

"Cancer's got it the worst," said Gemini, "but we call him Crabby."

"Crabby?"

"The zodiac sign for Cancer is a crab. And you'd be crabby too if your name was Cancer."

"Fair enough . . ." said Harriet.

"So anyway, Mom put a curse on the princesses," said the mole. "They have to come down here and dance with us. And when the spell is finally complete, our families will be united, and they'll have to come live down here forever." He didn't sound thrilled by the prospect.

"We can't talk about it," said August, returning. "Not to anyone who doesn't know about the curse already. I mean, we try and our throats close up." She did a brief jitterbug in place. "And we have to keep dancing and January *has* to put a sleeping potion into the hot chocolate every night."

"Is there a curse on you too?" Harriet asked Gemini. "Is that why you're dancing?"

Gemini stared at her. "You have *clearly* never met my mother."

"No, but I expect I shall," said Harriet.

The mole sighed. "We don't get a choice," he admitted. "Aries refused once, said he didn't want to dance, and she turned his claws into sponges for a week."

"Sponges?" said Harriet, baffled.

"It was horrible," said Gemini. "He kept trying to dig and all he did was get the dirt really, really soggy."

The hamster had to admit that this was ingenious. "So you don't like dancing either?"

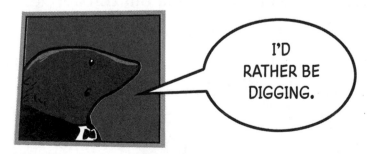

I'D RATHER BE DIGGING.

The mole hunched his shoulders defensively. "I love my mother and all, but I don't want to live with her forever! I want to travel! Go dig strange new dirts! Smell foreign rocks!" He sighed. "But the spell will keep us all down here, where she can keep an eye on us . . ."

And keep you dancing to power her spells, thought Harriet, but didn't say it out loud.

"I don't want to live underground forever!" said August. "I haven't even left the palace for years! I'm tired of being *stuck!*"

Harriet rubbed a hand over her face and turned to Gemini. "So if I can break the curse and deal with your mother, you and your brothers won't put up a fight?"

"Princess Harriet," said Gemini, "if you can convince my mother this is a bad idea, you will have my undying gratitude. Anything you want dug, we'll dig it. Anywhere. Anytime."

"I don't need anything dug," said Harriet. "Well, not personally—I have a friend with a flooded basement. I may get you to fix that, assuming we all get through this without getting married or turned into frogs or something."

122

She tapped a nail against her teeth and thought for a minute. "Is your mother watching us? Is she going to poof in here or something?"

"She doesn't really *poof*," said Gemini. "She's more of a tunnel-up-through-the-floor type. And no, at this time of night she's in a bubble bath with a copy of *Witchcraft Today*."

"Okay." Harriet nodded. "I have an idea."

WELL . . . MOST OF AN IDEA. A VERY SOLID BEGINNING TO AN IDEA, ANYWAY.

"Unfortunately, you're going to have to go in and dance for part of the evening, because otherwise it'll look suspicious. And don't tell anyone else I'm here. The more people know a secret, the less of a secret it is."

August looked at Gemini. Gemini looked at August.

WELL ... I SUPPOSE ONE MORE NIGHT CAN'T HURT.

Hand in reluctant claw, they went through the doorway and into the pavilion.

CHAPTER 10

Harriet woke up in the morning because a guard was poking her in the ribs.

He was using his finger and not a sword, so Harriet did not feel the need to shake him until his teeth rattled, but it was a near thing.

"What time is it?" she growled. "Is it even six o'clock? Why are you waking me up?"

"It is half past seven," said the guard. "His Majesty wants to see you. Immediately."

The mouse king sat on the throne, looking altogether too awake for this hour of the day. (Harriet's father, the king, slept until nearly noon most days, and stayed awake for half the night.)

I WAS HOPING THAT SOMEONE WITH YOUR CREDENTIALS WOULD WORK MORE QUICKLY.

"Yeah," said Harriet. "Remind me how long they've been doing this, again? Seven years, was it?"

The mouse king scowled. "Return here in the evening," he said. "You will have your three days. But then I want results, or you will be banished forever from the kingdom."

"How awful for me," muttered Harriet.

She actually would have liked very much to get on Mumfrey and leave the kingdom as fast as the battle quail could carry her.

But no. There was the royal hamster family's future to consider.

Harriet gritted her teeth. Even if the future hadn't been at stake, she really didn't want to leave the princesses in the lurch. Being trapped in a palace with the mouse king had to be pretty awful, even if he *was* their father.

She left the Throne Room and went through the Orange Hallway and a Blue Room, then fumbled her way through the Magenta Room with her eyes closed. Eventually she made it to the stables.

"Wilbur!" she called. "Wilbur!"

Wilbur came around the side of a stall, wiping his hands on a cloth.

WILBUR, I NEED YOUR HELP.

She produced a list. "I need you to go to the hardware store and get me everything on this list."

Wilbur took the list and read it over. "Hmm. Okay, I think I can do that after I'm off work . . ."

"Great. Bring it all to the Throne Room the day after tomorrow, early in the morning." She poured gold coins into his palm. "Thanks, Wilbur. You're the best friend a princess could have."

"Qwerk!" said Mumfrey from his stall. He was getting annoyed that Harriet was off having an adventure without him, and this was the last straw.

"Except for a battle quail, of course," Harriet added hurriedly.

"Qwerk."

"So you think you can save the princesses?" asked Wilbur.

"Huh? Oh, yeah. Sure. Piece of cake. It's the waiting," said Harriet. "I've got two more days of this. And I'm not sure it's going to go right. There's a whole bunch of ways it can go wrong."

Harriet was not good at waiting. Most of her adventures involved whacking things. She was very good at whacking things. (Also smiting, thumping, and general mayhem.)

But waiting . . . all she could think about was how easily things could go wrong.

If something went wrong when you were fighting dragons, you got set on fire, and that was very unpleasant, but at least you (and perhaps your faithful battle quail) were the only ones in trouble.

If something went wrong here, there were a *whole bunch* of people in trouble.

"Twenty-four of them," she told Wilbur. "Plus Mumfrey and me. Twenty-six total. We're only a thirteenth of the number of people in trouble . . ."

"I still think you have an unnatural love of fractions," muttered Wilbur.

"Yeah, yeah. But—c'mon, come outside the stable . . ." Harriet glanced around, wanting to make sure that no one was listening. "Look, it's not just us! It's the future of the hamster kingdom!"

She explained what the fairy shrew had said. Wilbur was fascinated.

WOW!
HOW DO YOU
SUPPOSE IT WILL
WORK?

"I dunno," said Harriet. "Maybe there's a horrible monster that shows up to eat the kingdom, and one of the mouse princesses' great-grandsons slays it."

"It's always slaying with you," said Wilbur. "What if your great-grandson is all sickly—"

"My great-grandson will have a *superb* constitution," said Harriet, miffed.

"—and one of the mice invents a cure?"

"It could be anything," said Harriet, who was secretly hoping for a monster. (Presumably she would be long dead, because otherwise she'd slay the monster herself. Harriet planned to be beating up ogres when she was ninety.) "Right, Mumfrey?"

Mumfrey wasn't listening. He was looking across the lawn, very distracted by a new arrival.

"Hi," said August.

"Oh, good!" said Harriet. "I was hoping I'd get a chance to talk to you."

August's riding quail, Hyacinth, was plump with very long eyelashes. Mumfrey pranced and tried to look taller.

QW-ER-ER-ER-K?

Harriet and August exchanged knowing looks. Wilbur rolled his eyes and went off to shovel things.

"Right," said Harriet. "Walk with me."

"I can't go very far," said August. "The guards will stop me if I get too close to the edge of the lawn. It causes earthquakes."

Harriet paused.

HOW LONG DOES IT TAKE FOR THE EARTHQUAKE TO START?

HARDLY ANY TIME AT ALL. I WALK TOO FAR AND THINGS START RATTLING.

EXCELLENT.

They made their way along the back of the stables. Mumfrey and Hyacinth continued to make eyes at each other.

"Can you talk to me about the spell now?" asked Harriet.

"I think so," said August. "It's different now that you *know*."

"So what have you done to try and break the spell?" asked Harriet.

"Everything," said August, groaning. "It all started when we were really young and Dad made *all* the girls in the kingdom take dancing lessons."

"Anyway," said August, "dancing was okay, but then at night we couldn't stop. We can't *not* dance. I mean, we can sort of stop for a few minutes, to get a drink or go to the bathroom, but it's like an itch, and you have to scratch eventually. And then the door started opening and we had to go underground . . ." She shrugged.

"What happens if you don't go?" asked Harriet.

"Can't," said August simply. "I've tried. I tied myself to the bed with a belt once. Lasted five minutes. The belt came untied and I danced a quadrille down the stairs. And a quadrille requires four people, so that was *not* easy!"

"Mmm. And if January doesn't drug whoever is trying to save you . . . ?"

August sighed. "Poor January. It's hard on her. I replaced the sleeping potion with water once.

The prince woke up and came charging down the stairs and fell in the river. And it *ate* him."

"I knew that river was up to no good," muttered Harriet.

HE REALLY WASN'T A VERY NICE MAN. HE KICKED HIS QUAIL. BUT I DON'T THINK HE DESERVED THAT.

Harriet was of the opinion that quail-kickers deserved whatever happened to them, but it didn't seem polite to mention it.

"Okay," she said. "I've got . . . about half a plan. Definitely more of a plan than I had last night." She rubbed her hands together. "How do you feel about climbing down very long ropes . . . ?"

CHAPTER 11

That night, the guards locked Harriet into the room with the princesses, and all thirteen of them listened as the big iron bar went *CLUNK* in the sockets.

There was a sad little sound in the room, the sound of a dozen mouse princesses sighing at once. Harriet scowled at the barred door and almost felt like sighing herself.

She walked to the little screened-off bed. Just like the night before, January brought her a mug of hot chocolate, and just like the night before, Harriet kept it in her cheek pouch and spit it all into the chamber pot.

Then she lay down in the bed with the Poncho of Invisibility wrapped around her shoulders and waited.

There was scuffling and a scurrying and the sound of a stone door opening. Harriet slipped out of the bed and snuck after the princesses.

Down the stairs they went again.

They crossed through the forests of metallic trees and this time, Harriet didn't break off any samples. When the boats pulled away from the dock, Gemini was the last one to leave.

"Got your lead underwear on tonight?" he asked cheerfully.

Harriet hurriedly climbed aboard. The mole grinned. "There it is . . ."

He poled the boat across the dark water. Harriet squeezed August's hand again.

She had almost two-thirds of a plan.

Well . . . three-fifths.

Definitely more than half, anyway.

AT LEAST FOUR-SEVENTHS OF A VERY SOLID PLAN . . .

When they reached the dock, Harriet slipped out of the boat. She was on her guard, in case Gemini was planning to double-cross her, but the mole pulled off his cloak, adjusted his tuxedo, and said, "Well?"

August looked around for Harriet, which would have worked better if Harriet wasn't invisible.

"I'm over here," said Harriet. "Okay. Gemini, day after tomorrow, I may need you and your brothers to do some digging."

REALLY?!

"Uh," said Harriet, who had underestimated how strongly moles felt about digging. "Yes?"

Gemini grabbed her by the arm, put his shoulder against her waist, and pulled. Harriet nearly decked him before she realized that the mole was trying to dance with her.

"You look like a mole dancing with a disembodied hamster head," said August. "It's *very* weird."

"Dancing is weird, if you ask me." Harriet disentangled herself from the waltzing mole. "Can you dig up into the castle?"

"Sure," said Gemini. "No problem. How fast do you want it done?"

"I can give you five minutes," said Harriet. "Will that be enough?"

Gemini drew himself up to his full height, which barely came up to Harriet's collarbone. "We're descended from a long line of mole witches and mole engineers," he said proudly. "We can do it in three."

THAT'S
FIVE-SEVENTHS
OF AN EXTREMELY
SOLID PLAN . . .

The next morning, Harriet woke up at half past seven, although the guard had the good sense not to jab her with anything.

"I'm coming," she said grumpily. "I don't know why. I get until tomorrow."

"We are growing impatient," said the mouse king when she arrived, rather frazzled, in the Throne Room.

"We who?" asked Harriet.

"It is the Royal We," said the rat advisor hurriedly. (The Royal We is what it's called when kings and queens refer to just themselves as "we" instead of "I." Harriet's parents had never done anything like that, and Harriet thought it was all rather silly.)

"Oh. Good for royal them," said Harriet. "Look, tomorrow morning, all right? I'm on the cusp of a major breakthrough here."

YOU THINK YOU KNOW WHERE THE PRINCESSES GO AT NIGHT?

"I am forming some ideas," said Harriet, backing toward the door. "Investigating leads. Gathering clues. I'll see you tomorrow, Your Royal We-ness."

She ducked out of the room and went down to the stables. Mumfrey poked his beak over the stall door.

"We'll be done soon, buddy," she told him. "Then we can get back on the road." She considered. "Well, or I'll have doomed my kingdom to some kind of horrible squishy future."

Mumfrey glanced over at the stall where Hyacinth was standing and said, "Qwerk," which is Quail for "No rush."

"Tomorrow morning, I need you and Wilbur to be under the tower with the princesses' bedroom," said Harriet. "It's the one with the bars on all the windows."

"Qwerk . . ." said Mumfrey, which is Quail for "That seems weird."

"Bring Hyacinth along with you," said Harriet. "It'll be easier." She stood on tiptoes and hugged him fiercely.

She spent the rest of the morning composing a letter home to her parents. It was a postcard of the mouse kingdom, so she had to write small and couldn't explain things very well.

Dear Mom + Dad,

I am in the mouse kingdom trying to break a curse. The mouse king is kind of a jerk and I don't trust him. If I wind up dead or cursed again, please make sure Mumfrey is well fed and look after Wilbur because it will be my fault he lost his job in the stables here.

Also, if I fail, the kingdom will be doomed in a couple of generations, so you should probably talk to somebody about that.

Love,
Harriet

She stared at the letter for a while and then added:

P.S. Do not worry.

She suspected that Wilbur would tell her that writing Do Not Worry on a letter about how she might wind up dead was not going to stop her mother from worrying, but she couldn't think of anything else to do.

"Life was easier when I was invincible," she muttered, and went into town to mail her postcard.

That night, when January brought her the hot chocolate, Harriet drank down every drop and went to sleep. She had a feeling that tomorrow was going to land like a ton of bricks and she wanted to be well-rested when it crashed down on her head.

CHAPTER 12

In the morning, Harriet was summoned before the mouse king at the unholy hour of five o'clock in the morning.

"This is ridiculous," said Harriet. "Doesn't the king sleep?"

"Four hours a night," said the guard. "He spends the rest of the time sorting the Royal Library by color."

"By *color?*" said Harriet, scandalized. "How do you find a book in it, if you don't know what color it is?"

"We've all stopped trying," said the guard, and opened the door to the Throne Room.

The mouse king and his rat advisor waited for her at the end of the hall.

WELL? HAVE YOU FOUND WHERE THE PRINCESSES GO AT NIGHT TO DANCE?

"Yep," said Harriet.

There was a brief, awkward silence.

WHAT, REALLY?

"Look," said Harriet, "I'd rather only tell this story once, and it's all tied up with the curse and whatnot. Can you bring everybody in?"

The mouse king inhaled sharply, but waved for the guards to bring the princesses. Harriet kept an eye on the door. It was *very* early in the morning . . . would Wilbur make it in time?

It is very awkward making small talk with a king while you wait for a curse to be broken. Harriet tried: "So, how about this weather we're having?" This earned her a deathly glare.

She looked at the door again. Still no sign of Wilbur.

"Err . . . color-code any good books lately?"

"Yes," said the mouse king. "Three green ones. They were lovely."

"What were they about?"

"They were *green,*" said the mouse king, as if it were obvious.

The princesses shuffled in, yawning. September leaned on May and snored.

"Now that we are all assembled," said the mouse king, "tell us what you have learned!"

"Right," said Harriet. "It's all very simple. At night, a magic staircase opens in their room and they go down it into an underground cavern full of magic metal trees, across a black river that's not quite made of water, and dance all night with the twelve sons of a mole witch. They're dancing on a symbol that I'm pretty sure is powering the mole witch's spells. Then they come back upstairs."

The mouse king stared at her.

"Do you have any proof?" asked the rat advisor.

Harriet reached into her pack. "Right here," she said, and pulled out the branch from the silver tree.

As Harriet had half suspected it would, when the king touched something from the kingdom underground, it had alerted the mole witch. The flagstones crackled and split. Up into the Throne Room emerged the head and shoulders of a gray mole with wild hair and a large pointed black hat.

"Who dares to challenge my spells?!" screeched the mole witch.

The mouse king drew himself up. "Who are *you*, madam?" he said. "And why have you cursed my daughters?"

I AM THE WITCH MOLEZELDA!

I AM THE MOUSE KING!

"I'm sure you'll get along great . . ." Harriet said to herself.

The Witch Molezelda folded her claws together and glared at the king. "It's not a *curse*," she said. "It's a *spell*. I have twelve sons and I required twelve brides for them."

"And why," said the mouse king acidly, "did you choose *our* daughters for this?"

"Here it comes," said Harriet, to no one in particular.

"I could have picked anyone," said Molezelda. "I just needed twelve dancing brides to power my magic."

("Thought so . . ." muttered Harriet.)

"But my sons are all named after signs of the zodiac," said Molezelda. "Your daughters are all named after months of the year. When I heard of them, it was obvious that they belonged together."

162

"Signs of the zodiac, you say?" said the mouse king.

"Sure," said Molezelda. "Aries, Gemini, Sagittarius, Virgo, Libra, and all the rest. A good, proper naming scheme." She nodded to the king.

"Ye-e-e-s . . ." said the king slowly. "Yes, it is." He turned toward the princesses, looking suddenly thoughtful.

Harriet cleared her throat. "About my half of the kingdom . . ." she said.

The mouse king ignored her. "Twelve months," he said. "Twelve signs . . . yes, of course!"

He stepped down from the dais, toward Mole-zelda.

YOU HAVE JUST GIVEN ME AN ANSWER TO A PROBLEM THAT HAS WORRIED ME FOR MANY YEARS, MADAM.

"I could swear that there was something about half the kingdom as a reward," said Harriet to his back.

"I have twelve beautifully organized daughters, but where would I find suitably organized men to marry them? What was the point of giving them such names, if they are going to go off and ruin it?"

UNLESS THEY MARRY EACH OTHER!

The twelve princesses took a step back. One or two of them burst into tears, but the mouse king didn't seem to notice. September had fallen asleep again.

Molezelda sniffed. "I didn't expect you to be so reasonable about this," she said. "Given that I plan to keep them underground forever and all that."

The mouse king shrugged. "So they'll be close by and can visit for holidays. I don't see the problem."

("Other than the eternal imprisonment bit?" asked Harriet, who was pretty sure no one was listening to her.)

"Clearly we should have talked sooner," said Molezelda. "Would have saved me some spellcasting."

"I could really go for half the kingdom about now," said Harriet.

The mouse king waved a hand at her dismissively. "*Your* services are no longer needed," he said.

OH, NO.
HALF THE KINGDOM
AND A ROYAL PRINCESS.
THOSE WERE THE RULES.
I'LL TAKE AUGUST, IF YOU
DON'T MIND.

"I'm, uh, not really interested in marrying you," whispered August. "No offense."

"It's fine," Harriet whispered back. "I'm twelve. I'm not marrying *anybody*. I just want to stop this plan."

The mouse king glared at Harriet. "The princesses are not available," he said. "It would break up the set."

"They're people," said Harriet. "Not a *set*." She glanced toward the door again, and was enormously relieved to see Wilbur's nose poking around the edge of the door frame.

"They're princesses," said the mouse king. "They will marry whomever they are told to marry."

YOU KNOW, I WAS FEELING A LITTLE BAD ABOUT WHAT I WAS GOING TO DO TO YOUR PALACE, BUT SUDDENLY I DON'T ANYMORE . . .

"Look," said Harriet, "we had a deal. You promised me half the kingdom and a princess! Are you
going back on your word?" She sniffed. "Some
king you are."

The mouse king went red in the face. "How dare
you talk to me like that, you insolent—hamster!"

GUARDS!
SEIZE HER!

CHAPTER 13

Guards poured into the room.

Harriet grabbed August's arm. "Run!"

The first guard was just a bit slow getting in their way. Harriet dodged around him and dove for the open doorway where Wilbur was waiting.

He had a burlap sack in one hand. He started to say something, but Harriet snatched it from him, saying "ThankyouWilburyouarethebestnowget-outofhere!" and tore down the hallway with August hot on her heels.

"Stop them!" yelled the mouse king, somewhere behind them.

They skidded into the Gray Hallway and saw guards at the end, three deep in front of the door to the outside.

Harriet hadn't really expected them to leave the door unguarded, but she'd been hoping. There were too many guards to fight. Somebody might get hurt.

It might even be her.

"Why did I ever stop being invincible?" she muttered, pulling August into a Blue Room.

She yanked the bag open and pulled out a can.

Three mouse guards dressed in Blues appeared in the doorway.

"Stop!" cried the first guard.

"In the name of His Majesty!" cried the second guard.

"The mouse king!" cried the third guard.

"Like I was going to *forget,*" snapped Harriet, popping the lid off the paint can—and splashed the paint toward the door.

The paint was brilliant purple, the color of a radioactive grape. It ran down the guards' blue clothes, over their blue armor, and stuck to their fur.

One tried to take a step forward and the other two grabbed him by the arms.

"We can't go into the Blue Room now!" said one.

"We'll *clash!*" hissed the second one.

IF THE KING CATCHES US IN ONE OF THE BLUE ROOMS LOOKING LIKE THIS, HE'LL HANG US UP BY OUR TAILS!

Harriet let out a sigh of relief.

"You thought of everything!" cried August admiringly.

"I hope so," said Harriet. "Now run! Before we run out of paint!"

She flung hot-pink paint on the guards that tried to chase them into the Green Room and bright blue paint on the guards coming through the doorway of the Magenta Room.

She poured vivid orange paint down from a balcony, onto the heads of two guards and a butler, who had the bright idea of wearing black. Since very few things go with vivid orange, the three were forced to take shelter behind a curtain and wait for someone to come back with a change of clothes.

At last, with only one can of paint to spare, the two princesses reached the staircase leading up to the princesses' tower.

"If we go up there, we'll be trapped," said August dubiously.

"Not quite," said Harriet. "Go! I've got a plan."

August ran up the stairs. Harriet ran after her, stopping only to pour the last can of paint (a particularly offensive shade of olive) down the steps behind her.

"What do we do now?" asked August as Harriet slammed the door to the bedroom closed. She could hear the locks and chains rattling on the other side, and wished she had a way to lock them.

"Bar the door," she said instead. "They'll be here soon."

"What do we bar the door with?" asked August, looking down the long gallery where the princesses slept.

FURNITURE!

Twelve narrow beds and twelve wooden trunks made a very effective wooden barricade. Working together, August and Harriet had three beds piled in front of the door by the time the guards came clattering up the stairs.

"Let us in!" shouted the guards, banging on the door. The door slammed against the pile of wooden bed frames . . . and didn't open.

"More furniture!" cried Harriet.

"I always hated this end table!" said August, flinging the hated table onto the pile.

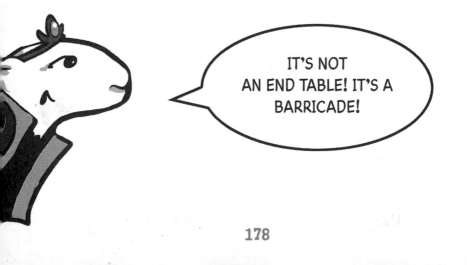

IT'S NOT AN END TABLE! IT'S A BARRICADE!

"August!" shouted the mouse king through the door. "August, you stop playing with that awful hamster and open the door *this minute!*"

"You want me to marry a mole!" August shouted back. "And he's an okay mole, but we're just *friends*, all right?"

"You'll marry whom I tell you to marry!" shouted the mouse king. "You'll understand when you're older!"

Harriet shoved the last of the wooden trunks into the pile of furniture. The mouse king was clearly not good at talking to his daughter. In fact, any minute now he was going to say—

"It's for your own good!" said the mouse king.

Harriet winced. *Nobody,* mouse or hamster or battle quail, likes to be told that something nasty is for their own good.

IF MARRYING MOLES
IS SO GREAT, THEN *YOU*
MARRY ONE!

August turned away from the door, her chest heaving. "I'm not marrying Gemini," she said angrily. "I'm *not*."

"That's the spirit," said Harriet. "Help me with this rope."

"Rope . . . ?"

Harriet pulled the last item out of the sack.

"A good rope," said Harriet, "is the adventuring princess's best friend. After a battle quail and a sword and a friend like Wilbur."

"Are we going to climb down it?" asked August. "But how do we fit through the bars?"

She glanced at the window. The space between the bars was not wide enough for even a very small mouse princess, let alone Harriet, who was a very solid little hamster.

Harriet tied the rope around the bars twice and secured one end to a bedpost. The other, much

longer end, she fed
through the bars and
out the window.

August frowned.
"But how—"

Something yanked
on the rope, twice.

Harriet grinned.
August rushed to the
window.

Forty feet down, Wilbur stood between Mumfrey and Hyacinth. He had finished tying the rope
to a harness, and gave a thumbs-up to August in
the window.

"You thought of everything!" cried August.

Harriet waved her hand. "This isn't my first adventure—" she began.

The floor heaved sideways.

August was thrown against the windowsill. Harriet caught herself and turned.

The trapdoor to the underground passage had appeared in the middle of the floor, and as they watched, the door began to rise.

CHAPTER 14

The enchanted stairs!" August gasped. "What do we do now?"

"Uh . . . ." said Harriet, blinking. "I hadn't thought of that . . ."

"But you thought of everything!" cried August.

"I think I'm doing pretty well, considering!"

The door opened wide enough for them to see the gleam of light from Molezelda's claws.

Harriet flung herself on the trapdoor, slamming it back down. There was a muffled curse from below.

"Open this door!" yelled Molezelda from the other side. "Open it at once!"

"Open this door!" yelled the mouse king from the hall.

"Do you want me to pull now?" yelled Wilbur.

"Do something!" yelled August.

"Will everybody *please* shut up!?" yelled Harriet.

Yelling at people to stop yelling is never very effective. The mouse king continued pounding on the door and Molezelda continued pounding on the trapdoor.

"Think, Harriet!" she told herself. "Think!"

(This is also not very effective.)

Fortunately, at that moment Wilbur decided he should probably be pulling. The rope snapped taut.

There was a *creeeeeaak* and a *groooooooan,* and a great deal of stone dust fell from the ceiling. For a moment it looked like the combined weight of two quails wouldn't be enough.

Harriet, realizing that she hadn't thought of everything, began to worry that she hadn't thought enough about *anything*.

"What is going on in there?" shrieked the mouse king.

The bars held. The mortar around them did not.

There was suddenly a gaping hole where the window used to be. August put her hands over her mouth in alarm.

The end of the rope that had been tied to a bed-post jerked taut and began pulling the whole bed toward the window.

"Grab that rope!" cried Harriet.

There was a loud thud from the door. The pile of furniture shook. August squeaked.

OH GOODY, THEY BROUGHT A BATTERING RAM . . .

THUD. THUD. THUD.

"Let us in," shouted the mouse king, "or we'll break the door down!"

Molezelda hammered on the underside of the trapdoor. "Open this door," she shouted, "or I'll break the floor open!"

BANG-BANG-BANG went the mole witch's claws on the wood.

"August," said Harriet very calmly, "now would be an *awesome* time to start climbing down that rope."

"Right!"

Harriet took a deep breath. She let it out. She counted to five, while the battering ram slammed into the door and Molezelda pounded against the trapdoor.

One . . . two . . . three . . . four . . .

The door fell off its hinges. The guards holding the battering ram ran into the wall of furniture. The mouse king screamed with rage.

Five!

Harriet dove off the trapdoor and ran for the window.

"Move these beds!" yelled the mouse king.

"Aha!" cried Molezelda, flinging the trapdoor open.

She emerged into the room just as the guards, still holding the battering ram, plowed through the furniture and ran right over the top of her.

SLAM!

URK!

"Where is that wretched hamster?!" shouted the mouse king.

"Oounnngggfff!" yelped Molezelda.

Harriet grabbed the rope, flung herself over what was left of the windowsill, and was gone.

"Are you all right?" cried Wilbur as Harriet climbed down the rope.

"Never better!" gasped Harriet. "Doing great! Get August on that quail!"

The mouse king's head appeared in the ruined window. "Stop her!" he shouted.

There was a brief confusion among the guards. Harriet decided not to risk matters, aimed for Mumfrey's saddle, and let go of the rope.

QWERRK!

"Sorry, Mumfrey," said Harriet, having landed hard on the quail's back.

Wilbur climbed onto Hyacinth and pulled August up behind him. "Now what?"

"Aren't you the stable boy?" asked August.

"He's also a prince," said Harriet. "A *great* prince. Best prince I know."

"Awww . . ."

"I'm not marrying you," said August, putting her arms around Wilbur and hanging on tight. "No offense."

"I'm really okay with that," said Wilbur. "No offense."

The guards were sliding down the rope now, having apparently decided against cutting it.

"As long as we've sorted out who's not marrying who," said Harriet, "let's ride!"

She squeezed Mumfrey with her knees and he took off across the lawn.

"Stop them!" shouted the mouse king from the window.

The ground began to boil. Molezelda erupted from the ground, looking very much the worse for wear.

BOYS! STOP THEM!

More mole hills appeared all over the lawn. Gemini popped up from one, looked at Harriet, looked at his mother, and said, "Err . . . stop who, Mom?"

"Them!" cried Molezelda. "Her! The hamster! And the mouse! *That's your future wife!*"

"She doesn't seem very interested, Mom . . ."

The two quails pounded across the lawn. More moles dug their way up through the grass, looking puzzled.

"Where are we going?" shouted Wilbur.

"I can't go far!" cried August. "There'll be an earthquake!"

"That's what I'm counting on!" said Harriet. "If you leave the area of the spell, I'm pretty sure it'll break! Otherwise why would she be trying to stop you?"

There was a surprisingly thoughtful silence for somebody riding a galloping quail.

". . . huh," said August. "Makes sense."

Guards ran after them. Moles converged on them.

None of them arrived in time.

Hyacinth the quail, carrying Wilbur the prince and August the princess, crossed some invisible line.

The earth began to dance.

CHAPTER 15

Harriet pulled Mumfrey to a stop, and Hyacinth stopped next to him.

It was a small earthquake at first. The guards looked around uncertainly. Slates rattled from the castle roof.

Harriet jumped down from Mumfrey and waved to one of the moles. "Which one are you?"

"Err, Aries, ma'am," said the mole, saluting. He seemed very confused by the entire situation.

Harriet didn't plan to give him time to figure it

out. "Get your brothers," she said. "Go back in the castle and pull everyone still inside into the tunnels. The tower is probably going to come down in a minute, and there may be some damage to the rest of the castle. Gemini told me you could do it in three minutes."

YES, MA'AM!

"We're going to knock the *castle* down?" said Wilbur, shocked.

"Well, probably not the *whole* palace," said Harriet. "The tower is where the magic's connected . . ."

"Yes!" said August, punching her fist in the air. "I hate that tower!"

The earthquake was starting to pick up steam now. A few rocks fell out of the walls and plunked to the ground. One of the lower windows—into a Blue Room, by the color—cracked.

It was obvious that the worst of the shaking was in the tower that held the princesses' bedroom. Stones were raining from the hole where the quail had yanked the window out.

"Hopefully we won't have to knock it *all* down," said Harriet. She cupped her hands around her mouth.

HEY! YOUR MAJESTY! EITHER YOU AGREE TO LET THE PRINCESSES MARRY WHO THEY WANT, OR WE BRING THAT TOWER DOWN AROUND YOUR EARS!

"I don't agree to this!" shouted the king out the window.

"Neither do I!" cried Molezelda. "Boys, bring me that mouse! Don't let her leave the bounds of the spell!"

There was an awkward pause. Molezelda looked around, adjusting her battered hat. "Err . . . boys?"

"They're getting everyone out of the castle, just in case," said Wilbur. "It's very noble of them."

"They're good boys," said Molezelda vaguely. "They always do what their mother tells them. Who are you?"

"Nobody in particular," said Wilbur. "Just a prince. Ignore me."

The earthquake was really rolling now. More windows broke. From inside the castle came a loud bell as somebody pulled the fire alarm.

Harriet gritted her teeth. "Come on . . ." she

said under her breath, "come on, Gemini, get everybody out . . . we can't knock down a palace full of people . . ."

Harriet had some very unusual notions of princessly behavior, but flattening innocent civilians was definitely *not* something princesses did. Even if the squishy future of the hamster kingdom was at stake.

She was very nearly sure, based on where the cavern had been located, that the tower was the only thing that would fall down, but if she was wrong . . .

A fountain of earth erupted next to them and Gemini came out, dragging a guard behind him.

"More in there," he gasped, and dove back into the earth, like a fish into water.

Wilbur and Harriet scrambled to the hole. The faces of a half dozen mice, covered in dirt, looked up at them.

Harriet counted the butler, a cook, and two more guards. She gave the cook a hand up.

"Stop that!" yelled the mouse king. "Get back here!"

"You can stop this!" shouted Harriet. "August, tell him!"

"I'm not going to marry Gemini, Dad! Get out of the castle!"

The shaking intensified. The mouse king clutched at the windowsill to keep his balance.

More moles came out of the earth, leading

more mice behind them. Princesses and guards straggled across the lawn, hand in hand.

Aries the mole looked around, saw Harriet, and saluted again.

EVERYONE'S OUT, MA'AM. EXCEPT THE KING.

"What now?" asked August, inching toward the palace. The earthquake slowed but didn't stop.

Harriet sighed. "When I said I was going to bring the tower down around his ears," she said, "I was really hoping to do it *metaphorically*." She waved August forward. The rumbling in the earth began to quiet.

"You can't tell me what to do!" screamed the mouse king.

I AM THE KING!

The princesses were coming toward them, gathering around August. Harriet looked from mouse to mouse.

They were all dirty from climbing through the tunnels, but on every face was an identical expression of determination.

"I haven't been out of the palace this far in years," said January.

"I've never been out of the palace," piped up December.

"Do you want to go back?" asked Harriet. "Because frankly, I'd just as soon knock the whole place down, but you live there. I think the spell will break if you go far enough from the symbol underground, but I can't swear the castle won't fall down first."

The princesses looked at one another.

A HOME YOU CAN'T LEAVE IS A *PRISON.*

Harriet smiled.

"Aries!" she called. "Gemini! Go get the king!"

"No, you don't!" snapped Molezelda.

Harriet drew in a breath. She'd almost forgotten the mole witch.

Molezelda pointed a heavy claw at the mouse king. "That man is the first person I've met who understands the importance of color-coding library books. *I* will get him out of that castle!"

And she dove into her burrow, while Harriet stood with her mouth hanging open.

"I thought she just wanted the princesses to power her spells," she said. "I didn't realize she'd be interested in the mouse king . . ."

On the other hand, she *did* name her sons after

the signs of the zodiac . . . maybe she and the mouse king were meant for each other.

It did not take very long at all. A determined mole witch can move through earth faster than a quail can run.

"You will get back here!" the mouse king was yelling. "And you will be grounded for the rest of your lives until the wedding and then grounded some more and then—*YRRRK!*"

(The *ynk!* was the sound he made when Mole-zelda came up through the trapdoor and grabbed him.)

September giggled.

The sound of the giggle had barely faded from the air when Molezelda delivered the furious, be-draggled mouse king onto the lawn.

"There," said Harriet with satisfaction. "Every-body's out."

The princesses looked at one another.

"C'mon," said August to her sisters, and all twelve of them joined hands.

They walked across the lawn, away from the castle.

The tower fell down behind them, with a crash that rattled windows a mile away, and not a single one of the princesses looked back.

CHAPTER 16

"You owe me three weeks' worth of wages," said Wilbur grumpily as they rode away from the mouse kingdom a week later. "They did *not* pay me."

"Hey, they owed me half a kingdom," said Harriet. "It's not like *I* got paid either. I mean, I was going to give it back to the princesses, but it's the principle."

All in all, it had seemed like a good idea to leave town as soon as the dust had settled. The twelve princesses were doing just fine. August was opening a florist shop and March was apprenticed to a master chef. May had gone off to train as an assassin in the next county over, which had horrified Wilbur and delighted Harriet.

January, it turned out, had been secretly engaged to one of the guards for over a year, and he had taken the youngest mice to his mother's house. (It was a very large house.)

WITH NO BARS ON THE WINDOWS. OR *ANYWHERE.*

January, as presumptive heir to the throne, had repealed the law about mandatory dance lessons, "to prevent future magical incidents." Harriet approved of this enormously.

The mouse king and Molezelda the witch might have had something to say about it, but they were spending their honeymoon repairing the castle. The tower's falling had damaged part of the main castle, so they were rebuilding, organizing everything first by color and then alphabetically. Molezelda's underground cavern had survived the earthquake and she was paying for the reconstruction effort with silver trees.

"It'll keep them occupied for years," Gemini told Harriet a few days later. "But . . . err . . . we're all going to find our own patch of dirt while they're busy. In case they get any ideas." He tugged on his snout. "You might want to go too. Mom's in love with the mouse king, but she's got a long memory."

This was extremely good advice. Harriet took it to heart.

She'd left a note with August to keep an eye on Molezelda. If the mole witch got the idea to power her spells using unwilling dancers again . . . well, August had promised to send word.

Harriet nudged Wilbur. "It was time to leave anyway. Heady's egg will hatch soon. Besides, you got a battle quail of your very own. That's got to be worth something."

Hyacinth preened. Mumfrey made besotted qwerking noises at her.

"It was nice of August to give her to me," Wilbur admitted. "I suppose you don't have much time to ride quail when you're a florist."

"We didn't do so bad," said Harriet cheerfully. "You got a quail, I saved my kingdom's future . . ." (Gemini had also promised to take a look at the basement of Wilbur's castle, but Harriet was keeping that as a surprise.)

They came over the rise and saw an ancient shrew sitting by the side of the road.

"Princess Harriet!" called the shrew, waving.

Harriet reined in the quail. "Oh, it's you," she said. "I wondered if you'd show up again . . ."

"Indeed," said the shrew, fixing her with one bright eye. "Indeed. The mouse king didn't give you a reward, did he?"

"Well, he let me leave the kingdom without

throwing things at my head," said Harriet. "Does that count?"

The shrew fairy snorted. "No."

"But my kingdom's okay now? Not going to fall in a handful of generations, however long that is?"

"It looks okay," said the shrew. "I mean, it's still squishy, but it's a better sort of squishy."

"Well, that's a relief."

The shrew nodded. "We've taken the liberty of punishing Molezelda," she said. "She probably hasn't noticed yet, but she won't be able to borrow anybody else's power ever again. If she tries, her fur will all fall off."

"Yeesh!" said Harriet. "Why didn't you do that before?"

"Had to catch her in the act," said the shrew, shrugging. "And it might have been a little tricky if she had all those dancers to call on magically. But never mind that! I have come to reward you, Princess! For your valor in breaking the spell and freeing the mice and moles from bondage! And also to take back the Poncho of Invisibility."

OH . . . THAT.

"You lost the Poncho of Invisibility, didn't you?" said the shrew.

"I had a lot on my mind!" said Harriet. "There were people yelling and battering rams and more yelling and things falling down! I think I did very well, considering!"

"Those don't grow on trees, you know," said the shrew. "We can't just hand them out like candy."

"Sorry," muttered Harriet.

The shrew studied her for a minute, then her expression softened. "Well, you did do very well. Considering. A lot of other heroes wouldn't have done as well. I admit, pulling half the castle down was a little extreme—"

"It was only a quarter of the castle! At most!"

"—but it taught the mouse king a very good lesson," finished the shrew. "So I'm giving you a gift."

"Eh?" said Harriet.

The shrew beckoned. Harriet drew closer to the ancient fairy. "Kneel, hero," intoned the shrew.

The shrew reached out, tapped Harriet's crown, and said, "I grant you a very limited charm. You can cliff-dive again safely."

"*Really?*" cried Harriet. "*Cliff-diving!?*"

She could have hugged the old fairy, but the shrew vanished in a puff of smoke that smelled like cupcakes.

Harriet hopped up onto Mumfrey's back, grinning from ear to ear. She could cliff-dive again! Nothing could ruin her mood, although Wilbur did try.

"I can't believe you lost the poncho," he said.

"How will they find it? *It's invisible!*"

"The mouse king will probably find it and alphabetize it or something." Harriet waved her hand. "Who cares? I can cliff-dive again!"

Mumfrey set off, chirping. They passed a small clump of blue flowers by the side of the road, which neither of them noticed. Thirty years later, August, by now the queen of florists, would come by and collect the seeds. She would grow the seeds in her garden, and a handful of generations hence, Harriet's great-great-granddaughter would give them to a dragon in return for a very important favor.

But that's another story, and the future is always squishy.

In this time and in this place, atop two very happy quail, Harriet and Wilbur rode away into the sunset, and on to the next adventure.

THE END

DON'T MISS THESE OTHER URSULA

MOKING HOT BOOKS FROM
VERNON!

HARRIET'S FIRST
ADVENTURE!

HARRIET HAMSTERBONE IS A STAR!

★ "MOVE OVER, BABYMOUSE, THERE'S A NEW RODENT IN TOWN!"
—*SCHOOL LIBRARY JOURNAL,* STARRED REVIEW

★ "HARRIET IS HER OWN HAMSTER, BUT SHE TAKES HER PLACE PROUDLY ALONGSIDE BOTH DANNY DRAGONBREATH AND BABYMOUSE. CREATIVELY FRESH AND FEMINIST, WITH LAUGHS ON EVERY SINGLE PAGE."
—*KIRKUS REVIEWS,* STARRED REVIEW

★ "A BOOK WITH ALL THE MAKINGS OF A HIT. READERS WILL BE LAUGHING THEMSELVES SILLY."
—*PUBLISHERS WEEKLY,* STARRED REVIEW

★ " A JOY TO READ, AND WE CAN ONLY HOPE THAT HARRIET—LONG MAY SHE REIGN—WILL RETURN IN LATER INSTALLMENTS."
—*BOOKLIST,* STARRED REVIEW

ABOUT the AUTHOR

Ursula Vernon (www.ursulavernon.com) is an award-winning author and illustrator whose work has won a Hugo Award and been nominated for an Eisner. She loves birding, gardening, and spunky heroines. She is the first to admit that she would make a terrible princess.

VERNO   **FLT**
Vernon, Ursula.
Of mice and magic /

04/16